MW00964159

SALLY! SALLY! SALLY! SALLY!

BY

PAUL M. COOK

Sally! Sally! Sally! Sally!

ISBN Number 0-615-12048-2
Hardcover

This book was printed in the U.S.A.

For inquiries or to order additional copies of this book, contact:

PMC BOOKS & MUSIC
P.O. Box 706
801 Cheever Avenue
Geneva, IL 60134 USA
www.pmcbooksandmusic.com

ACKNOWLEDGEMENTS

Over the years, suggestions from my writer's groups, past and present, have been of enormous help — a word change here, a freshly slanted paragraph there. Many of these writers have become my close friends. Let me just mention the *groups*, my friends will know who they are.

Batavia Writer's, Batavia, IL; *Marilyn Robinson, Facilitator.*

Naperville Writers, Naperville, IL; *(The whole gang.)*

St. Charles Writers, St Charles, IL; *Rachael Tecza, Facilitator.*

St. Charles Library Writer's; *Rick Holinger, Facilitator.*

Concord Writers — Waubonsee College, *John Buckley, Facilitator.*

SOMEWHERE IN TIME

Very special thanks to the many hundreds of ***Somewhere in Time*** fans and *INSITE members* (International Network of Somewhere in Time Enthusiasts) from all over the world who I've come to know since I played the small part of Doctor Hull in the romantic movie. Thanks for your friendship, for liking my music, for encouraging me in my fiction efforts, and especially for the roars of laughter we've shared each year at The Grand Hotel, Mackinac Island, Michigan. *You're the greatest!*

And, of course, special love to my children — ***Tom, Grady, John and Lisa, and my step-daughter, Kimberly.***

FOR SUSAN

CONTENTS

I'LL REMEMBER APRIL

The first Sally story

CHAPTER 1

I'LL REMEMBER APRIL

I saw her from a distance, fifty yards I guess. I had to squint but I knew it was Sally. Some things you know with certainty, even after so many years. I suppose I would have recognized her anywhere on earth.

Perhaps it was the angle of her body that I remembered, or the way her short ponytail fluffed from beneath the flat-brimmed straw hat. Maybe it was her profile, blurred, of course, from that distance.

But I knew it was Sally. I knew it.

I walked slowly. As I got closer I saw that she was wearing sunglasses. A dog was stretched out beside her — a large cream-colored Labrador Retriever with a dark muzzle. It lay quietly beside Sally in the shadow of a long wooden bench mounted to the boardwalk several feet above the sand.

Then I noticed the dog was wearing a special, heavy-duty harness with a leather grip-handle resting on its back. After a moment I realized I was not breathing — I was holding my breath. *Sally was blind.*

She faced into the breeze, out toward the sand and surf of the Atlantic. The brim of her hat kept the sun from hitting her face directly. I moved closer. Her arm stretched down beside the bench and she stroked the dog with the back of her fingers. I heard her call him Barney. He licked her hand several times then settled his head back down on his paws.

As I passed, I glanced at her face. She hadn't changed much. Her hair was still light brown, pulled back and bound with an elastic band of some kind, the way I remembered it from so many years ago. But now her ponytail had streaks of gray.

She was such an attractive woman — a handsome

woman. I searched my memory. Sally was sixty-seven years old. That made me sixty-eight. (You forget sometimes.) She was slim and shapely — *still had those great legs.* Her breasts filled out her short-sleeved polo shirt perfectly. She had certainly lost none of her appeal.

Sally sat still and erect, and though her eyes were hidden by the sunglasses, I remembered them as greenish blue, always laughing, always kind. *Kind blind eyes,* I thought.

Her tanned arms told me that she was accustomed to the sun, probably from walking the beach with Barney. A sudden gust of wind caused her to remove a tissue from her straw handbag and blot her eyes from beneath her glasses as blind people sometimes do.

I took several steps beyond her and stopped. A seagull squawked and floated nearby on the breeze looking, I suppose, for bits of popcorn, scraps of pretzel, or pieces of hot dog bun.

Down on the wide, white St. Augustine beach, children screeched and made mad dashes away from the shallow waves that chased them, their bare brown feet making imprints in the wet sand. "Don't go too far," mothers called. I turned and looked back at Sally, staring at her for almost a minute.

"May I help you?" I heard her say, still facing straight ahead toward the ocean.

"I'm sorry," I said, startled, "I was just standing here watching the children." The gull squawked again and soared off down the beach.

"I felt your shadow," Sally replied.

My shadow. My God, I thought, *she felt my shadow.* I fumbled for words. "Sure a nice day. Mind if I join you?"

"Not at all." Sally made the customary adjustment of shifting a fraction to one side so that a person felt welcome to sit. Barney lifted his head for a moment and eyed me.

I sat several feet away from her so she wouldn't sense that I was invading her space. My arm rested on the back of the bench. "The kids are playing tag with the waves," I said.

"Yes, they always do."

"You from down here?"

"For many years."

"I'm from up north."

She smiled and nodded. "I could tell from your voice." And then she repeated "— your voice."

I glanced down at her hands and saw the wedding band. I slouched. The thought that she might be married had crossed my mind, I guess, but I had dismissed it, foolishly.

We continued our conversation, talking about the weather, the hurricane season, the wild fires. "Nature's way of cleaning house," she said. Then, after a long silence (and kind of out of the blue) she said, "Have you ever pretended you were blind?"

"No, I guess not." I felt awkward.

"It makes you think differently. Try it when you get back to your motel. Just close your eyes and think of what you heard here today at the beach — the gull, the children, the waves. You'll be able to see things more clearly."

We small-talked for a while and later she said, "If you're getting hungry there's a little hot dog stand down the board-walk." She pointed. When I asked if I could bring her any-thing, she said she was fine, that she'd had a big breakfast.

I walked down to the stand and waited in line. *Wedding ring? Married?* I must have been crazy. Standing there in the April sun I felt an overwhelming letdown, but what the hell did I expect? I'd just head back north tomorrow and not say anything. Why stir things up? Another one of life's romantic ideas gone sour.

Balancing a hot dog, chips and drinks, I walked back down to her bench. "I brought you an iced tea," I said. "Four sugars."

Her lips parted and she turned her head quickly in my direction. I realized what I had said. How could I have made a slip like that? How could I have possibly remembered such a trivial thing as "four sugars?" But, I had.

I took her hand and guided it to the Styrofoam container. Tears welled in my eyes. I knew she knew. She'd probably suspected all along. I sat down beside her again and was quiet for a moment. "How have you been, Sally?"

"Not too bad," she said. "I've been pretty good." She pressed her lips together, her chin quivered. I helped her place her tea on the bench and she raised the tissue back to her cheek. They were real tears this time. "And you?" she asked.

My hand slid along the top of the bench until it touched her shoulder. "I've missed you."

"I've missed you, too."

We cried a little then, as true friends and old lovers sometimes do after a long absence.

"I decided to come looking for you," I said. "There's a place on the Internet that tracks people down." She smiled and took a long, broken breath. I hunched over and pulled a stem of grass from the sand. Resting my elbows on my knees, I twisted the stem with my fingers and stared out at the ocean.

"We got screwed up all those years ago, didn't we? Somewhere along the line we got screwed up — drifted apart."

"We were young."

"I guess so." I felt depressed and tugged another stem of grass from the sand. "I've thought about you, Sally. Always."

"And I've thought about you."

"I figured that if I ever found you again, maybe we could hang out together. Do stuff, you know. But I see you're married." I leaned back and tossed the stem of grass onto the sand. "It seemed like a good idea at the time."

She patted Barney and sipped her tea. "My husband

died several years ago."

"Good!" I said. *The word jumped right out of my mouth.* A burst of laughter from Sally. She couldn't help herself, I guess. I was embarrassed.

CHAPTER 2

Later, Sally, Barney and I took a long walk down the boardwalk to an open pavilion with a corrugated tin roof. I ordered cold drinks and Sally went into the ladies room with a woman she knew from the neighborhood.

"Sally and I live in the same condo complex," the lady said when they returned. She pointed in the direction of a group of single story, blue-framed buildings on a rise behind a line of low sand dunes. The woman glanced back toward the ladies room and said to me under her breath, "I check things out for her before she goes in."

Sally and I sat at a metal table beneath a bright red canvas umbrella for what seemed like hours, peeling back the years. I told her a few jokes. She liked jokes. We talked easily, and laughed a lot, as if we'd never been apart. The umbrella fringe flapped in the breeze and Barney snoozed.

"When I was flying down here," I said, holding her hand and stalling for courage, "I was hoping that if I found you, and things turned out, maybe we could kind of, well, stay together. That is if you were interested." I paused. "You know, give it a try." God she was pretty.

Sally had never been shy. She was open. She spoke her thoughts. "I don't think it would work."

"Why?"

"I need a certain amount of attention — a certain amount of being taken care of."

"I'm not busy."

"You wouldn't like it."

"You never know. I might."

We let it slide.

The old guy working the counter tuned his radio to a *Golden Oldies* station. From beside the table, Barney watched Sally and I dance. And the few people who were seated at other tables also gave us sidelong glances, curious to see a man dancing with a blind woman, I guess.

The radio played *Long Ago and Far Away,* and then segued into *I'll Remember April.* Sally was smooth and confident. "April is when we met," she said.

"April? Was it? That's right, I remember."

"Liar."

I smiled and pressed her to me. God, *she even smelled like April* — fresh and young like early spring.

In case you're wondering, Sally was the first intimate romance I ever had.

Some people think men don't give a thing like that much thought, but it's not true. Some of us do. We're the romantics. How could I possibly forget the fumbling uncertainty, the thrill and excitement, the tenderness and beauty of my first love? No, I'll never forget. After all, first loves only happen once in a lifetime.

And as we danced, our bodies touching, our shoes sliding smoothly across the sandy cement floor, I still felt that same love, that same passion that we once knew. So, it was only natural, I guess, that I somehow maneuvered the conversation around to the subject of sex.

"Sex?"

"Why not?" I said. "I just figured, you know, that if we still have something in common — if we still care for each other a little — I mean —"

"I don't think you understand —"

"Understand? Sex? I might be a little rusty but I *understand."*

She smiled and shook her head, "It's not like when we were young — the old days. It's not as simple as —"

"Blind people have sex, don't they?"

Sally shrugged. "I wouldn't know. I've only been blind a few years. I suppose they do."

"You bet they do. You don't have to see to have sex. What's the matter with you? It's like breathing. Most people keep their eyes closed anyway. Nothing to it."

"You'd probably peek."

"Yes," I said, "I probably would."

There was another one of those long silences between us. The song was ending. "Well," I said, "what do you think?"

She pressed her hand on my back, her cheek against mine,

her breasts moving softly against my chest. "Okay," she said quietly, releasing her breath into my ear. That word was exciting enough all by itself, but then she added one more, "When?"

I kissed Sally right then and there, holding her in my arms at that rickety old pavilion on the beach.

Barney raised his head. The people at the tables tried to hide their smiles. They knew they were watching two people falling in love. And, we were. Sally knew. And I knew. It all came rushing back.

I squinted across the dunes toward the blue condos. "How do we —"

Sally took my hand. She leaned down, and with her other hand she found the leather harness and grasped the handle. "Barney knows the way."

— This lovely day will lengthen into evening —

CHAPTER 3

I finally bought half of the condo and moved in. That's the way she wanted it—everything fifty-fifty. I did a little painting, twisted new light bulbs into most of the lamps, and added a few framed watercolor landscapes to the walls. The place looked nice. For my birthday she was able to get me a round of golf at a very prestigious country club. She rode on the cart with me even though it was against the rules.

I drove her to her doctor's appointments and for her weekly manicure. Afterward, we'd often drive on down the coast to a little Mexican place we liked and have a couple of drinks — some tacos, beans and rice. Sally ate rice with a spoon, kind of secretly pushed it on with her finger. With a fork it would fly everywhere. Usually we'd split a bottle of wine and after I paid up we'd break a few speed records getting back to the condo.

You'd have laughed — me trying to get her clothes off and my clothes off at the same time. I'd get overanxious I guess, and so would she. And her bra — *her brassiere!* Honest to God, if I live to be a hundred I'll never get the hang of those things.

I'll tell you one thing, herding an oversexed blind woman into the sack with a Labrador Retriever cold-nosing you and banging its tail back and forth is a challenge — a full-time job. You've got to keep your mind on business.

But later, snug under a sheet and cotton spread, listening to the low, steady hum of the air conditioner, Sally in the darkness of her world, and me (her protector) holding her hand, feeling her next to me and watching through the window at the clouds creeping past the moon, I realized — *that's about as good as it gets.*

CHAPTER 4

One sunny day we got married. It was casual. The members of the condo association got us a big cake and we had hamburgers and drinks out by the pool. Barney had a field day—probably gained fifteen pounds.

That night we all partied around a bonfire on the beach until Barney took us home.

CHAPTER 5

A year, six months and sixteen days, that's what we had — one Christmas, one New Year's and one wedding anniversary.

CHAPTER 6

Barney and I — we sit out at that old wooden bench on the boardwalk a lot these days, looking out at the Atlantic. He doesn't wear his heavy harness anymore and he's hard of hearing. We both walk a little slower and we grunt when we stand up.

We listen to the children squealing and watch them running from the waves. Old Mr. Gull comes zooming by, screeching and raising hell, and then goes soaring on down the beach and out over the marsh.

Sally was right. If you close your eyes and just listen, thinking of what you hear, you're able to see things differently, more clearly somehow — and you remember. I do that almost every day now, and feel her shadow.

... I'll remember April...

AN AFTERNOON AT HARRY'S

The second Sally story—
different time, different place, different Sally

AN AFTERNOON AT HARRY'S

I suppose Harry's New York Bar in Paris, France, is as good a place as any to reflect. Those of us who drink alone a great deal of the time do that, you know.

We sit hunched over the bar and squeak the rim of our glass with a finger or make little designs in the amber whiskey spilled there on the surface, and we reflect: flashes of memory, small bursts from the past.

If you're young, you might not think those flecks and bursts of memory amount to a hill of beans, as Bogart said in one of those great scenes from *Casablanca*. But they *do*. Because, for some of us, *that's all we have.* That's all that's left of a lifetime — those little flashes — those little bursts of memory.

So, here I sit in Paris, alone at Harry's New York Bar. A business trip. It's a nice place, really — a shrine, like Westminster Abbey. Ernest Hemingway and F. Scott Fitzgerald and Gertrude Stein — they've all been here. It's where they invented the Bloody Mary, the French 75, the Sidecar. Why, just imagine all the yarns and stories that must have started here at Harry's — right at this very bar.

Well anyway, I guess I should tell you that I've been sitting here this afternoon thinking about something that happened a long, long time ago.

You see I didn't have to take the seat right next to her on that airplane. It's so obvious when you do a dumb thing like that. I mean there were other empty seats — whole rows of empty seats. But, I'd had a few, and I felt just right, exactly right — *adventurous.*

So I plunked myself down beside her. I learned that her name was Sally. Sally, of all things. She was so damned attractive — dark brown hair and eyes, friendly smile, light brown tailored suit.

"Join me for a drink?" I managed. Now I ask you, how's *that* for an original get-acquainted opener? She was quiet and reserved. Me? I was on top of my game. I was funny, really funny. And finally I made her laugh. She ordered wine.

Three more stops and she'd be getting off in Memphis. Tulsa for me. A puddle jumper. I was meeting someone. She was meeting someone. There's a certain safety in knowing you'll only be with a person for a few hours. You have the freedom of going beyond the norm. You'll never see them again. You gamble.

Several drinks later, I realized I was no longer trying to be funny. I was serious. The warmth of good whiskey spread through my body. You've probably been there yourself. Everything you say has a special grandeur. Your words take on metaphysical proportions. Whiskey.

Then, suddenly, we were looking into each other's eyes and talking about life and about love and about two people together. And as melodramatic as it might seem, we were both out there lost in the stars somewhere. It's the truth. I felt no one else existed in the universe but the two of us — no moment in my life could be as pure and as true as that moment.

And after a while, as we talked so seriously, Sally held the back of my hand to her breast. That's all, nothing more. No one could see us. And I said, "I love you." And she said, "I love *you*." And we meant it. We really did. It just happened, that's all. Oh God, it was grand.

Well, that's what I've been thinking about this afternoon at Harry's New York Bar, letting the warm whiskey do its melancholy job. And to this day, I say to myself, "If there is a heaven, that was as close as I'll ever come to it."

So, I squeak the rim of my glass and draw little designs in the amber liquid here on the bar. I wonder how things like that happen once in a lifetime. I watch laughing people come and go, and keep gazing at the door, hoping, I suppose, that by some miracle of miracles, Sally will be standing there. And like an old movie, the patrons will fade and disappear into swirling clouds. Sally will come forward and look into my eyes. She'll press the back of my hand to her breast and say,

"I love you."

But, that was then and this is now, as they say. It's getting dark — dreary day turning to dreary evening — and it's beginning to rain. Better be on my way.

I suppose you've guessed by now that Sally didn't make it this afternoon to Harry's New York Bar in Paris, France — nor to the hundreds of other places over the years.

Maybe tomorrow.

SALLY & TOM

The third Sally story —
different time, different place, different Sally

Sally and Tom is an excerpt
from Paul Cook's novel,
A Change In Plans.

SALLY & TOM

The first few days working on a movie set were always fun for Tom. He would often bump into fellow actors he had not seen for months, sometimes years. He enjoyed the great, rousing hel-los, the dirty jokes and bullshit stories. He liked hanging out with the production crews, who were always equipped with biting humor, and not greatly impressed with actors one way or the other.

He found a space for his car in the hotel parking annex, and decided to pinch pennies. He'd leave his suitcases in the car, check in, and come back for them later. No bellboy, no tip. Being broke was not for the timid.

He meandered between the big movie trailers at the far end of the lot: trailers for wardrobe and props, trucks that housed camera equipment, lights, reflectors, generators and electrical cable. There was even a *honey wagon* for toilet facilities. License plates told him that everything had been brought in from Los Angeles.

Three identical Chevrolet Cameros were roped off and parked side by side. Chase cars, he reasoned. If one got banged up, there was always a replacement. That's how he was able to get his Jaguar. It had been damaged several years before in a movie chase scene when it glanced off a curb at high speed. Bobby, his production manager friend, arranged for a little creative bookkeeping and at the end of the shoot Tom bought the repaired Jaguar for next to nothing.

In the lobby it was noisy, and crowded with actors, extras and members of the crew. Their T-shirts and windbreakers read, *The Galveston Bay Story — A Phantom Films Production.*

Passing the gift shop he heard his name called. "Tom! Tom Mitchell!" His heart skipped. He knew it was Sally.

When he turned, there she was, Sally Farrachi, waving to him from beside a hotel wall phone. "I see an old friend," he heard her say. "I'll call you back."

They hurried toward each other, Tom grinning, stretching out his arms. "Sally, Sally, Sally." Her eyes sparkled. Tom lifted her several inches off the floor and slowly spun her a full turn before easing her back down and hugging her. She felt good — soft and warm and familiar. The light trace of her perfume he remembered well.

"Twenty years between hugs," Tom said. "Aren't you a sight."

"It's so incredibly incredible," Sally said. "What in the world are you doing here?"

"The Judge. I'm playing the Judge. His smile widened. "I just can't believe it. And what are *you* doing here?"

"The hooker. I'm playing the old hooker. Not the young one, I'm dreadfully sorry to say."

Tom held her hands up to his chest, smiling into her eyes. "Age doesn't matter, Sal, it's the thought that counts."

"Not much of a part," she said. "After I get laid I get murdered."

"Whoa!" Tom chuckled. "Could be worse, I suppose. Could be the other way around."

Sally punched at his chest. "Same old Tom."

"And what's all this?" he said, reaching out and fluffing the bottom of her hair, "you're a blond."

"Dyed it to get the part." She pursed her lips and modeled dramatically, turning her head from one side to the other. "Beautiful, don't you think?"

Tom stroked her cheek with the back of his fingers. "Yes, beautiful."

She had always been beautiful to him, by any standard, a blend of French and Italian, which Tom assumed produced her gray, smoky eyes. "I also have a cultural pinch of British aristocracy from my mother's side," she once told Tom.

"The pinch of American bullshit," Tom countered, "must come from your father's side."

Tom and Sally first met when they were paired at a commercial audition in Chicago for a breakfast cereal. Tom eyed her closely, watching her respond to the director and clients. She laughed easily and often, and had a quick, appealing delivery. She got the part. So did Tom.

He learned that she was adored by most of the directors and film crews, not because she was such an exceptional actress, but because she was a hard worker, never complained, remembered her lines, and was such fun to be around. She would often be hired for small parts simply because she was *Sally*.

A week after filming the commercial, Tom coaxed her phone number from the talent agent, inviting her to join him for lunch at the *London House.* They drank gin Gimlets far into the night. Later, at her small apartment on Scott Street near the Ambassador East Hotel, he learned that beneath all of her snappy humor and bubbling enthusiasm, she was quiet and gentle and tender.

That's how it started. They had an affair that summer. Their *torrid* affair, Tom called it. Their *horrid* affair, Sally would say, and pinch his fanny. Everyone who knew them hoped they would get married. The perfect couple. It didn't work. One day Sally stopped drinking. Tom didn't.

"I heard you got married," Tom said. They moved a few steps to a small alcove beside the gift shop. "A rich doctor or something."

"Patent attorney," Sally said. "Nice guy. You'd like him. We live in New York now." Sally patted Tom's hand. Her eyes narrowed and she lowered her voice. "And I hear you were in the hospital."

"Yes, I was."

Sally waited for a moment. "So?" she said finally, "don't just stand there. How are you feeling? How are you doing?" She looked at him seriously. "You know."

He shrugged, "Too soon to tell, Sal. Haven't been put to the real test. But at least I haven't had a drink in a couple of months. I quit smoking, too."

"I'm so glad, Tom, so very glad. I've worried about you." Her eyes widened. "*Meetings!* Have you been going to meetings?"

"I've been to the Mustard Seed a few times."

Actually, he had attended several other AA meetings in Chicago at various locations. They seemed to be everywhere. He felt comfortable at the Mustard Seed, knowing he was rubbing elbows with some world-class alcoholics. "Someday they'll retire my chair," Tom said. "Hang it from the rafters."

"I'm glad for you, Tom." Sally took his arm and pulled

him through the crowded lobby toward the coffee shop. At the entrance, Tom stopped. "Wait," he said, and lifted her hand above her head. "Lets have a look at you." She pivoted slowly as he looked her up and down. "You look wonderful, Sal, just wonderful." He leaned to her and whispered, "Have I told you lately that you've got the greatest ass in North America?"

"You used to include South America."

"Of course," Tom said, "South America, too."

"You ought to know," she said.

Tom wondered if he detected sadness in her smile. In the coffee shop, Sally forced Tom into a booth, ignoring his complaints. "For Chrissake, Sally, I've got to go to the front desk and register, then find the Production Office and tell them I'm here."

"You can register later," she said firmly, "and the people in Production are having a meeting. Besides, I haven't seen you in all these years." She leaned forward and put her elbows on the table, her chin in her palms, her gray eyes wide. "I want to schmooze. I want to know what's going on in Chicago. I want to know who's screwing who—whom. Every last detail."

They talked about *the old days,* the talent agents, casting agents, unions, people in the business who had been their mutual friends.

"The London House finally closed," Tom said. "There's a Burger King there now."

"I don't believe it."

"Ricardo's changed hands."

"Ricardo's?"

"They might tear it down."

Sally was silent.

"The Boul Mich is gone," Tom said. "The Surrey, the Ink Well."

"It's sad," Sally said. "I thought the *London House* was in the National Register."

They often drank late at the London House, Sally sitting on a high barstool down at the curved end of the bar, Tom standing beside her, his foot resting on the rung of her chair. They would listen to the jazz of Oscar Peterson or George Shearing or Marion McPartland, always close, always touching—a hand resting on a shoulder or a thigh or a knee. When Sally had enough to drink she would blink slowly, slide her fingers down behind Tom's belt buckle and rock him back and forth against her. And in the darkness of the bar, with George Shearing playing Avalon, she would kiss him wetly behind the ear. "Let's go to bed," she would whisper.

"Yep," Tom continued, "they're all gone, all the old haunts. It's like somebody shot my dog."

"It'll get better, you'll see."

Tom leaned back in the booth and stared at her for a moment. "We were quite a pair, weren't we? The two of us."

"Yes, quite a pair."

The waitress warmed their coffee as they reminisced — a weekend in New York, lunch at Knickers, and an afternoon at the Village Green. At Knickers they had seen a movie star having lunch at a nearby table.

"He looked right at me," Sally said. "He smiled at me."

"Right."

"Well, he did."

"What he was looking at, Sally, were your tits. That's what he was looking at."

Sally raised her eyebrows. "Maybe he was and maybe he

wasn't. But, then," she paused, "so were you." She leaned across the table, their faces almost touching. "And I've got a little surprise for you, Mr. Know-it-all, so was the bartender."

Their eyes gleamed — danced — as they smiled at each other.

"I'm afraid we got a little tipsy that afternoon," Tom said.

"A little?"

"The bartender over-served us. What the hell was his name?"

"I haven't the faintest idea."

"You told him you'd remember his name for the rest of your life."

"We knocked over a tray of strawberry desserts. I remember that."

"My God," Tom said. "I guess we did." He rested his arm on the back of the booth, remembering that when they left *The Village Green,* Sally had taken off her shoes and rested them in the crotch of a tree.

"We waltzed," Sally said, "on that dirt path in the middle of Central Park."

Tom smiled and nodded, knowing that she was remembering the past at the same time he was.

"I lost my shoes," Sally said, frowning. "And then over on 59th Street, with all those people watching, we waltzed again."

Tom pictured her beautifully shaped bare feet moving skillfully on the sidewalk.

"Me barefoot!" Sally continued. "Waltzing!" A smile of remembrance crossed her face. "Right there in front of the Plaza Hotel, New York, New York."

Tom remembered that when they stopped dancing he continued holding her in his arms, looking into her eyes as pedestrians hurried past them.

"You kissed me," Sally said. "Just like in the movies. People applauded."

The waitress slid the check onto their table. Sally looked down and slowly stirred her coffee. "I thought my heart would burst that weekend."

"I thought mine would, too, Sal."

They were quiet for a moment.

Tom said, "I've been thinking about you, you know."

"About me?"

"A lot."

"I don't believe it."

"I've wanted to tell you something. I've wanted to tell you goodbye."

"Goodbye?" Sally frowned again. "You going someplace?"

"No, I don't mean that. I mean I just wanted to say goodbye, you know, in case something ever happens to me and I don't get a chance to say it."

Tom remembered the helplessness he felt one stormy day looking out of the hospital window at a young woman, a perfect stranger, who dropped her car keys in the parking lot. He still pictured her stooping and searching for them in a puddle with her bare hands as the wind blew and the rain poured down on her. He put his hand to the window and cried as he watched her.

He remembered the many times tears rolled down his cheeks as he talked to his friend Ida, the psychologist. Tears welled in his eyes now. He shook his head slowly as he gazed at Sally. "People don't get a chance to say goodbye sometimes, that's all."

"You planning on jumping off a building or something?"

Tom reached across the table and held Sally's hands. They were soft and smooth. He rubbed the pads of his thumbs on each of her polished nails as he talked. "When I was in the hospital," he said, "I realized there were a few people who have passed through my life who were important to me. I mean, really important. People I want to say goodbye to, you know, just in case I up and croak one of these days."

"And I'm one of them?"

Tom squinted. "One of them? Of course you're one of them. How could you even ask such a question?" He searched for words as he held her hands. "You know what I mean. There was something very special between us — a special feeling — a special friendship. Things we liked in common."

"Sex."

Tom blushed. "I didn't mean that, but that too, of course."

"A special — love?"

Tom stared at her. "Yes, I suppose that was it, a special love."

Sally blinked back tears of her own. "Funny you were never able to say that word before."

"No, I guess not. I don't know why." He continued to

hold her hands. "It doesn't happen very often in a lifetime," he said, "that special feeling for someone. I just wanted you to know. It's important for me that you know."

Sally took a deep breath. "In case you weren't aware of it, I've always loved you, too." She looked away. "Maybe just a little bit more." She paused and glanced back down at the table. "Why don't you get married, Tom? Find somebody. Settle down. Marriage is not so bad, you know."

"Who'd have me?"

"I would have, once."

Tom cocked a smile. "You never asked me."

"Dammit," Sally said, easing her hands from his grasp. "Why do you always foul up what is meant to be a compliment with a stupid joke?" She brushed a tear from her cheek. "Yes, I asked you. I asked you in many, many ways."

Tom took her hands again. "I'm sorry, Sal. I'm really sorry. It *is* a compliment, a true and wonderful compliment. I don't know how to behave sometimes with compliments."

She wiped at her cheeks with a napkin. "It's all right. Let's not fight. We've got three whole weeks. We'll have fun. If we get some time off we'll go to a few meetings together. Okay?"

Tom smiled and squeezed her hands. "Okay."

She looked at Tom with her sad, gray eyes. "No horsing around," she said. "Deal?"

Tom nodded. "Deal."

* * *

The meeting with Bobby, the production manager, happened fast, lasting for less than ten minutes.

Standing in line at the registration desk, Tom saw him sitting with two men in the lobby. The men had their backs to Tom. Bobby stood up and waved. He motioned for Tom to join him at cushioned chairs on the other side of the room.

After handshakes, they sat down and talked. Bobby's face was troubled. He twisted a rolled-up film script in his hands as he spoke. "I'm sorry, Tom. I don't know what to say. God Almighty, nobody knew where you were. Couldn't find you anywhere. Couldn't get ahold of you."

Tom felt a great tiredness. He slumped down in his chair. "My fault," he said. "I should have called from on the road."

"It happened overnight," Bobby said. "All of a sudden a

new director, a new producer. Nobody told me. I had no idea. You better call Lisa," Bobby said, referring to Tom's daughter. "She's frantic. She thought maybe you had fallen off the —"

"Yes, I'll call her."

The lobby crowd was thinning out. Muffled laughter came from the two men sitting on the other side of the room. Tom exhaled, looking in their direction. "Who's the new director?" he asked, squinting across at them.

"Blazak."

Tom let it sink in. "Producer?"

"Conrad."

"I see." He pursed his lips and nodded. "Well, it figures. Makes sense, I guess. I had a little run-in with them." Tom looked Bobby in the eyes. "Booze."

"Yeah, I heard." Bobby paused. "You can stay here at the hotel, Tom. They'll pick up your room for the three weeks."

Tom gritted his teeth and then shook his head.

"Why not?" Bobby asked, frowning. "Look," he argued, "don't worry about them footing the bill. Don't be noble. They've got the money. Your bill is a drop in the bucket. Besides, it's in your contract." Bobby removed an envelope from between the pages of the twisted script. "Or, if you don't want to stay here they'll pay you in cash. Either way."

Tom rested his elbow on the arm of the chair, his fingers to his forehead, staring down at the carpet. It would be no good staying at the hotel. It just wouldn't work. He'd find another place. Maybe even drive over to New Orleans for a few days and look for a job as a deckhand on a freighter or cruise ship — begin writing that novel he'd been thinking about. If he was smart he would take the cash, get a room at a cheap motel and have enough left over to get his brakes fixed.

Tom looked across the lobby toward the coffee shop where he and Sally had talked. Beside it was another public room. *Gulf Side Bar,* the sign read.

Bobby spread his hands pleadingly. "Tom, listen to me. They can't just up and fire your ass. Take the money."

There were more muffled chuckles from across the room. Tom glanced up. The two men were looking his way. He took the envelope.

"Your cancellation check for the job itself will go through the Guild," Bobby said. "You won't lose anything, unless maybe you would have gotten a little golden time, a little overtime. So, you'll get the same money, you see?"

"It's not so much the money, Bobby." Tom looked straight ahead, eyes fixed. "I wanted the job. I wanted to work."

Across the lobby the two men stood up. Bobby glanced at his watch. "My God, I've got to go, Tom. We're setting up for streetwalker scenes tonight. Hookers." He stood. "I feel awful, Tom. Just awful."

Tom got up and looked at Bobby's stricken face. He nodded. "I know you do, Bobby. You're a good man. When are you and my daughter going to get married?"

Bobby's eyes widened. "Holy Christ, I forgot to tell you. I called her this morning and asked her."

"What did she say?"

"She said okay."

"Good. That's good." They shook hands. "Marriage is not so bad, you know," Tom said.

* * *

The lobby was empty. Tom stood at the entrance to the

Gulf Side Bar, his hands in his pockets. He looked down at the carpeting and nudged at a clump of dirt with the toe of his shoe. After a moment, he turned and walked to the front desk and asked for stationery. He sat at a small writing table near the windows overlooking the lawn and the Gulf of Mexico.

Dearest Sally,

There's been a hitch—a little change in plans. Bobby will explain. I'll see you in New York one of these days. For sure. I'm looking forward to meeting your husband. I mean it. He's a lucky, lucky, lucky guy. And remember this, Sal. Please remember that I love you. Always have and always will.

Knowing you, loving you, has been something very special in my life.

Tom

WHAT NOW, MY LOVE?

The fourth Sally Story —
different time, different place, different Sally

CHAPTER 1

SEX

Sally did not suffer from nymphomania. Not at all. She was just an ordinary girl who liked ordinary sex. *A lot.* Made no bones about it.

We were both writers at the same ad agency in Chicago. She was smarter, a better writer, and so damned attractive — *seductive.*

We used to make love until I thought my ears would pop. You know, like when you go up and down in an elevator or an airplane. Not kinky stuff. (Well, maybe just a little now and then, *at my urging.*) But mostly, just everyday, down-home, no frills sex.

Tornados could be uncorking monster-assed trees from the ground, ripping shutters from hinges, peeling sheets of shingles from roofs, and Sally would just lay back, pretty as you please, lips moist and parted, gray eyes half closed, bare heels spurring my fanny, with her own made-in-heaven rear end pumping away like the City of New Orleans rumbling through Memphis.

When the smoke cleared, Sally was soft and warm and tender. Her smile? — *a gift.*

And I was in love with her.

CHAPTER 2

THE ART OF SWEARING

Sally was born at Ft. Belvoir, Virginia, her father a colonel in the army. I don't like the term "army brat" but she did travel with her parents all over the world before they settled in the outskirts of Chicago.

Her two brothers were rough and tough and, as you might expect, swore a great deal. In fact, the whole family swore a lot, Sally's mother included. I met them all at a wedding reception one weekend at Ft. Sheridan, Illinois.

I was crazy about Sally's mother — Italian and small

like Sally, with a great smile and a booming laugh. She told jokes with the best of them.

Sally's father was Irish. He, too, was quick with a laugh, but somewhat more reserved. He didn't shy away from a drink though, and told limericks and sang bawdy songs all the way back to town, with Sally embarrassed, rolling her eyes and stretching out the word, "Dad."

Sally's mother sang right along with everybody else. Knew all the words. I guess the whole family had an influence on Sally's swearing. Pros. Swear words rippled off their lips as smoothly as if they were reciting Shakespeare or the Lord's Prayer.

Of course, when it comes to swearing, I'm no slouch myself.

CHAPTER 3

AUTHOR'S ADVICE

As a writer, Sally told me to avoid words such as *hyperbole, oxymoron,* and the dreaded *proletariat*, saying that using such words displayed only conceit, arrogance and, in the long run, ignorance.

Using such words, Sally claimed, red-tagged you as a boring asshole.

CHAPTER 4

THE SOCIAL CLIMBER

Sally didn't like parties, but she went this once to please me. And who happened to be there but this guy Stafford, the *lady-killer*, the *brain*, who worked at the same ad agency (different floor) as we did.

"Yo, Stafford," I said. *(I despised him.)* He had a big-bucks Caribbean tan, wore cutoffs and Jesus sandals. A world class jerk. When I introduced them I could tell right away that Sally didn't like him. I figured there might be trouble. I was right.

A few drinks later he made a pass at her, using his phony

Ivy League lingo. He was vulgar, very vulgar. Ever notice how the pseudo intellectuals and the very wealthy are often the most vulgar? *I mean deep down in their hearts, vulgar.*

The room was crowded and I had my back turned, but I learned later he had wet-kissed the nape of her neck and slid his hand down the backside of her jeans, then up between her legs.

Sally's voice was rarely loud. But now, it came alive, from way down deep. Guttural rumbling — an exorcism. Now came her art of swearing. *"You sonofabitch! You prick of nature! You scumsucker!"*

My gal Sal.

My head spun around. Party conversation not only lagged, it came to a standstill. Hell, I didn't even know what had happened.

For a small woman, Sally packed a big wallop. She smacked ol' Stafford's golden face hard, very hard, like a wet towel slamming a flat rock. She didn't back away, not an inch. He rubbed his reddening cheek and then clinched his fists. For a moment I thought he was going to hit her. I took a step forward.

He didn't hit her, he hit me. *Broke my goddamn jaw!*

They wired me up at the hospital and she took me back to her place. Her kisses were feathery that night, lightly brushing my lips so that she wouldn't hurt me. Her touches were soft and, later, her movements agonizingly slow.

CHAPTER 5

THE NURSE

For a week I basked (Sally says "basked" is phony) lazily on her couch while my jaw healed. We watched old movies and she gave me long rub-downs and held thick malts under my chin so I could suck them down with fat straws.

Sometimes we'd put a quilt and pillow down on the floor and have sex, trying to take it easy so we wouldn't disturb the old folks in the downstairs apartment.

With my jaw wired, I had trouble forming words. "Wook out bewoe," I said one afternoon as we stretched out on the quilt. Sally got a laughing jag. She couldn't stop. Tears streamed down her cheeks. She'd catch her breath, double over, and start laughing all over again, ending, I'm sorry to say, what might otherwise have been a rather exciting sexual encounter.

As the days passed, every now and then I would catch Sally staring at me with a special kind of affection that I'd never noticed before. A glow. It was embarrassing.

One afternoon, with that peculiar look, she said, "Thanks."

"Thanks for what?"

"Oh, I don't know, thanks for being you. Thanks for protecting me. Thanks for being my hero."

And I finally realized that what she was talking about was that hesitant step I had taken toward Stafford the night he broke my jaw.

Sally smiled at me. It made me feel good. It made me feel strong. I probably blushed.

She got up and spread the quilt, tossed down the pillow, and slipped out of her robe.

CHAPTER 6

HER BUSINESS TRIP

I wonder where you are now
Now—this very moment
A drug store
A coffee shop
Out there so far away in San Francisco
Is it cold, is it damp like they say
Are you taking care of your asthma
I think of what a lifeless life
Life would be
Without you
I picture you sitting across from me now
Here in our special booth
Your hand on mine
My hand on yours
Your hand on mine again
Playing our silly child's game
God, I love you
I miss you

CHAPTER 7

SMALL VICTORY

Then one day we're on the commuter train into Chicago. Jammed. Standing room only. Parents and teachers screaming their brains out at children screaming *their* brains out, heading down to Navy Pier or the Air Show or something.

Lo and behold, who are we standing right next to — shoulder to shoulder — Stafford. Stafford, the jawbreaker.

Sally freaked out. She started whispering in my ear with her lips not moving, like a ventriloquist, "Don't say anything. Pretend he's not here." She held my sleeve. "If you start anything the cops'll yank you off the train and throw you in the slammer." She sometimes used old movie words like that. I'm thinking, *Like I'm going to pick a fight with the guy who busted my jaw a month ago when I can just as easily hide behind a tree someday and smack him over the head with a goddamn two-by-four?* Women complicate things.

So, I thought I'd be cool, let bygones be bygones, turn the other cheek and all that bullshit.

"Yo, Stafford," I said. *(I despised him.)* "How's the novel coming?" Now I thought Sally was going to faint, keel right over, me talking to him. I could see it in her eyes.

Stafford was a technical writer at our agency, (automotive upkeep and safety tips) the prick. On the side he was moonlighting, writing a sci-fi novel he kept hidden in his desk drawer about a monster snail that hauled himself up out of Tokyo Bay every night and ate all the Japanese in a path eleven miles wide. Plowed right down through Tokyo and Yokohama and on into the outskirts of Osaka, with crazed Japanese men, women and children, their arms outstretched, running for their lives yelling "hubba-hubba" and shit like that. Can you imagine?

They blasted the snail with everything, from bazookas to the hydrogen bomb. Kid stuff. Old Mr. Snail was going to devour the entire planet. Stafford was the laughing stock of the agency.

I repeated myself. "How's the novel coming, Stafford?"

Stafford gave me an expressionless look. He was leery. "It's coming okay," he said.

Sally got up her courage. "And how is the weasel?"

Stafford drew himself up tall and frowned. "It's not a weasel, it's a snail."

"Of course," Sally said, her expression saying *how could I have made such an incredible error.* "And how is the *snail?*" she persisted, digging away at Stafford. And I'm thinking Sally's gone a little nuts herself, standing there in front of passengers talking about a goddamn snail chewing up Tokyo, just like the snail was alive and well and reading the Tribune up on the observation deck.

"He's okay," Stafford said to Sally.

"Well, it's one hell of an idea."

Stafford brightened. "You think so?"

"Bet that mother-huncher is big."

"Very big." Stafford's eyes sparkled.

Sally leaned to one of the teachers. "He's writing a novel. Monster snail eats Japanese." The teacher nodded, turned and screeched at children swinging from the baggage racks above.

The train finally slowed and came to a halt at Northwestern Station. The door slid open. Sally took a step down, then leaned back in. "Tell the weasel we said 'hello.'"

"Snail."

"Right." Sally gave him a thumbs-up. "Tell him we said 'hi.'"

On the station platform, Sally pulled me behind one of those huge I-beams. We were laughing. She kissed me and said, "I love you," as Stafford, head down, plowed through the crowd like a fullback.

CHAPTER 8

PILLOW TALK

"Do you think Stafford is good-looking?" I asked.

"Stafford?"

"Yeah."

"Good-looking?"

"Yeah."

"I guess, kind of. Why? What brought that up?"

"I just wondered."

Sally rolled over on her side and faced me, her arm bent at the elbow, head resting in her palm. "I'll make this short," she said. "I'm tired, and we have to catch the early train.

Stafford is an asshole. The girls up on his floor think he's an asshole. I can't stand him, they can't stand him. He's rude, conceited, arrogant and loud."

The sheet fell away from her breasts. They jiggled, adding emphasis to each word as she gestured. "He's a bully," she continued. "You think all the women like Stafford and Stafford likes all the women, right? Wrong. Why are you asking this anyway — some kind of stupid jealousy thing?"

She flipped the sheets, got out of bed and stood naked, looking down at me from the shadows, hands on hips. "God, you're dumb. Stafford doesn't like women. He hates women. He feels threatened — feels women are not his equal. Stafford is good-looking but he's an asshole. You're good-looking and *you're* an asshole. But I love *you. Get it*?"

She got back in bed and pulled the sheet up. "Good night." She turned away from me. We lay quiet for a long while until she whipped the sheet off once again and got out of bed.

"What's the matter?"

"I've got to pee, that's what's the matter."

When she came back to bed she slipped her arm beneath my neck, looking into my eyes. "Hell, maybe it's me," she said. "Maybe *I'm* the asshole." She leaned over and kissed me lightly on the cheek. "You piss me off."

I didn't say anything. I just rested my palm on her bare hip until I heard a deep sigh and finally the soft, steady rhythm of her breathing. I kissed her shoulder.

CHAPTER 9

LUNCH BREAK

W*e got married. City Hall.*

Everything planned down to a split second. Our boss, Harry, the agency copy chief (a pal of mine) was the only one in on it. *Super secret, so Sally wouldn't find out!* He'd worked on it all week. Said we had to be back at the agency by 2 P.M. — major client meeting. No excuses.

How Harry did what he did (blood test, marriage license, etc.) I've never to this day figured out. All I know is he went to high school with the mayor and was one of the groomsmen at the mayor's wedding.

Out on Wacker Drive, I pulled Sally into the back seat of a banged up old taxi and held her hand. I had never asked anyone before so I had never gotten a yes or no. I was nervous. I said, "Let's get married."

She said, "Why not?"

"I'm serious."

"I know."

"Your destination, sir?" The cab driver spoke with an East Indian accent, like Sam Jaffe in the old Gunga Din movie. He even looked the part and wore a small, faded turban, baggy pants and sandals. The cab smelled sweetly of incense, and was decorated with ball and tassel fringes, religious icons dangling here and there.

Sally and I dashed into Tiffany's on Michigan Avenue while Gunga Din circled the block a few times. (I think Harry had slipped him some extra dough and told him to hang around as long as it took.)

A fancy place, Tiffany's. She picked out her ring, a plain gold band, and her wedding present, a necklace with a small 24 karat gold cross. She had pointed it out to me a hundred times before. I'm not into religious gifts but she was happy. Kissed me right there in Tiffany's in front of everybody. She said I blushed, but she lies sometimes.

To City Hall!

We were dressed fairly well because of the client meeting. On orders from the mayor I guess, a cop was waiting for us in front of City Hall. Gunga Din was scared and confused. He jumped out and opened the cab door for us, bowed like we were dignitaries and shook hands with the cop.

The policeman hurried us down a maze of hallways and into a darkly paneled room. I looked at my watch. 1 P.M. A woman in a nurse's uniform took our blood samples and the cop rushed them out to a squad car. I heard the siren.

Sally spent her time looking at old black and white political photos mounted on the walls. She was interested. She studied them, saying things like, "Gosh, look at this." I paced, nervous and fidgety, twisting and squeezing my hands together until we heard the siren again and the cop came banging back in with the test results.

A moment later a clerk breezed into the room followed by the mayor and several of his office staff. They were all smiling. I thought Sally was going to keel over.

The mayor handed me a small white box with a ribbon. He shoved a card in my hand. It read, "Her corsage, stupid." It was signed — Harry.

I pinned it on her and suddenly the ceremony was over. I kissed the bride, the mayor kissed the bride, and the bride damn near wet her pants. The City Hall photographer even took a few pictures. There was applause and flowers — a floral arrangement from the Office of the Mayor, and an armload of roses from Harry. Outside, the little turbaned guy was still there, shooting the breeze with the cop.

A wild ride to the office, Gunga Din blasting away on the horn, swerving in and out of traffic and swearing, (in Hindi, I guess) at other cab drivers who were calling him a motherfucker.

My friend, Harry, raised his eyes to me as Sally and I eased into our chairs at the conference room table with the clients. 2 P.M. exactly. Harry had heavy eyelids and rarely smiled. I gave him a slow nod, like a hit man who had just rubbed out a rival from across town. Harry eased his glance over to Sally's ring, and then up to me, solemnly nodding back, like a Don.

I felt good.

CHAPTER 10

PILLOW TALK 2

"Did you know I was going to ask you to marry me?"

"Sooner or later."

"How?"

"Women know. It's a woman thing."

"Were you excited? I mean, with the mayor and everything?"

"Yes."

"So was I."

"I know."

By now I was kissing her breast. She whispered in my ear, "You're a little dense, you know. A little slow. I would have married you the first day I met you."

"I love you so very much."

She held my head to her chest, combing my hair with her fingers. "Yes, I know. I love you, too." We were quiet in each other's arms for a long time.

"Wook out bewoe," she whispered later.

CHAPTER 11

HONEYMOON

The night we landed in Paris we had dinner at the restaurant in the Eiffel Tower. Eiffel Tower? Don't laugh; the food was great and the view like no other. *The City of Light — and love.*

We wandered Paris for a few days holding hands and doing tourist stuff, walking along the Seine and having a drink at Harry's New York Bar where famous writers used to hang out. (I later sold a short story about the place.) The bartender bought us a drink. Sally and I danced over and over to the old French song, *What Now, My Love*? We laughed and drank wine, and when we tired of dancing, we wandered back to our hotel and made love.

We walked everywhere, and one afternoon she prayed at the Notre Dame Cathedral, fingering her gold cross as she came out. Back at our hotel we laughed, drank more wine and made love again, and I remembered the line — *all this and heaven, too.*

Finally we rented a Fiat and drove down to the Riviera where the rich folks stay. Then we spent a few days driving through the Alps, and at last into a little Italian border town where Sally's mother was born.

Sally called her in Chicago. The connection was bad. "We're in Italy," Sally said loudly. *"Italy!"* She threw up her hands *Italian style* and yelled into the phone. *"Where you were born, goddamn it!"*

Loving Sally was an adventure.

Her eyes softened and shifted to mine. She reached out and held my hand. "Yes, very," she said into the phone.

The working class town was beautiful, set high in the mountains, with good food and wine to warm us, but the altitude was tough, trudging around town trying to find a druggist to replace Sally's asthma inhaler. It was brisk, and she was catching a cold. Beneath giant quilts, we snuggled close that night, bodies touching, skin warm.

* * *

On the plane we held hands and took turns sleeping with our heads on each other's shoulders all the way back across the Atlantic.

CHAPTER 12

WHAT NOW, MY LOVE?

A lot of people from the office were there and, of course, Sally's mom and dad and brothers. Believe it or not the mayor ducked in for a moment and stood with my boss, Harry. Even Stafford was there, quiet and respectful. He shook my hand, I shook his.

But the thing that knocked me for a loop, almost brought me to my knees, was glancing into a shadowed corner of the room and seeing the little man in the faded turban and baggy pants looking into my eyes. Gunga Din. He bowed so gracefully, and then was gone.

I never dreamed of Sally dying
It never entered my mind
The coffin seemed so small
Like a child's coffin
And she looked like a child
She wore her ring and her
Gold cross
And I wanted to crawl in beside her
And close the lid
Oh God, Sally